What If ...?

A Margaret K. McElderry Book

ATHENEUM 1976 *New York*

What If . . . ?

Fourteen encounters—some frightful, some frivolous—
that might happen to anyone. J O S E P H   L O W,
in words and pictures, provides fourteen sensible solutions.

a token for
FLORENCE
and
DEL

Library of Congress Cataloging in Publication Data

Low, Joseph,   What if...?
"A Margaret K. McElderry book."
Summary: Describes how to behave in situations such
as being invited for a swim by a shark.
[1. Wit and humor] I. Title.
PZ8.7.L6Wh   [818]   76-12465
ISBN 0-689-50064-5

Published simultaneously in Canada by
McClelland & Stewart, Ltd.
Manufactured in the United States of America
Printed by Connecticut Printers, Inc., Hartford
Bound by A. Horowitz & Son/Bookbinders
Fairfield, New Jersey
First Edition

What if you were hiking across Africa
with your little brother and you
met a lion as big as a house?

Offer him half of your brother's chocolate bar.

What if you went to the zoo
and the monkey asked,
"How do you like
my neighbor?"

Say, "Just bearly."

What if a friendly dragon offered
to heat up your breakfast roll?

Go for the morning paper and say,
"Please call me when it's ready."

What if a tiger knitted you a pair of socks
forty-seven times as big as your feet?

Call your brother and say, together,
"Clever, Tiger! What a really marvelous
pair of sleeping bags."

What if a Martian wanted to marry you?

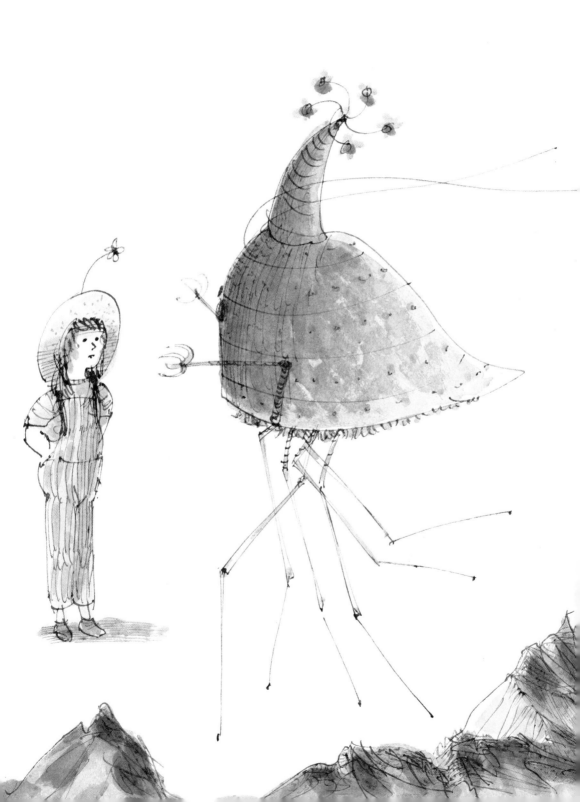

Give him your bike and say,
"I'm sure you'd be
much happier with my sister."

What if your dog, Zebulon,
brought you a basket of
new little robins?

Go out and buy him a copy of *Group Singing Made Easy*.

What if you were
writing a note to
your friend, Susie,
and a flying fish
came through the window?

Ask him to deliver it on his way back to the sea.

What if you were walking
through the woods some night
and there was a big, full moon,
and you heard an owl,
right behind you, say,   "Who?

Whoo?

Whoooo?"

Walk a little faster and say,

"Not me!

Not mee!

Not meeee!"

What if Blackbeard, the pirate,
invited you to go for a walk?

Smile and say,
"After you,
my dear captain."

1.

What if the prize in
your Cracker Jack box
turned out to be
a dinosaur that grew...

2.

and grew...

and grew?

3.

Say, in your politest voice,
"Would you care for some of
my Cracker Jacks?"

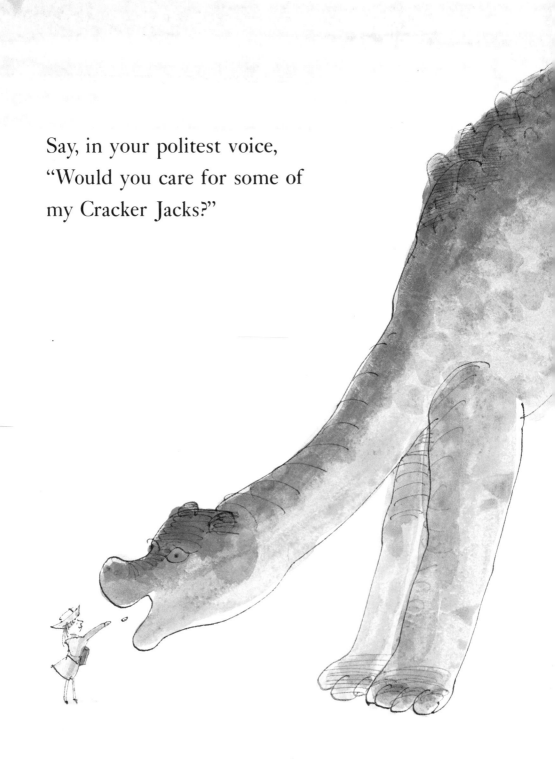

What if you were
fishing for minnows
and a shark said,
"It's such a nice day!
Come for a swim!"

Throw him a minnow and say,
"Thank you kindly,
but it's a little too
close to lunchtime."

What if Tough Tommy's goat ate up half your garden?

Stamp your foot and say,
"How could he do that...
without any
salad dressing?"

What if you were passing a cemetery in the dark
and you heard a sad voice moaning,

"Who stole my head?"

Ask, "Witch one?"

What if an elephant sat down on the other end
of your seesaw, without even asking?

Call your mother and father and sisters
and brothers and uncles and aunts and cousins
and Mr. Murphy, the policeman, and the boy who
delivers the papers (not the big one but the medium-
sized one) and your friend, Terry, and all her relations,
and that would balance him nicely.